© Matt Campbell 2004
First published 2005
ISBN 1 84426 068 8

Scripture Union, 207–209 Queensway, Bletchley,
Milton Keynes, MK2 3EB, United Kingdom
Email: info@scriptureunion.org.uk
Website: www.scriptureunion.org.uk

Scripture Union Australia, Locked Bag 2, Central Coast
Business Centre, NSW 2252, Australia
Website: www.scriptureunion.org.au

Scripture Union USA, PO Box 987, Valley Forge, PA 19482, USA
Website: www.scriptureunion.org

British Library Cataloguing-in-Data
A catalogue record of this book is available from the British Library.

Printed and bound in Great Britain by Creative Print and Design
(Wales), Ebbw Vale

Cover and internal illustration by Celia Canning
Cover and internal design by Hurlock Design

Scripture Union is an international Christian charity working with churches in more than
130 countries, providing resources to bring the good news of Jesus Christ to children,
young people and families and to encourage them to develop spiritually through the Bible
and prayer.

As well as our network of volunteers, staff and associates who run holidays church-based
events and school Christian groups, we produce a wide range of publications and support
those who use our resources through training programmes.

Contents

Introduction

Part 1:

The
Origins
of
Snot

Part 2:

JOURNEY
TO THE
CENTRE
OF THE
NOSE!

Part 3:

More Big Truths
About Snot
And *Why*
It Is How It Is

Part 4:

BOUNCING
BACKWARDS
AND
FORWARDS
IN TIME

Introduction

Ladies and gentlemen, boys and girls, brought for your education and enlightenment straight from the Department of Incredibly Serious and Highly Specialised Research at the University of Snot, it's **Professor Abednego Smott**, one of world's leading Snotologists, and a world-renowned specialist in the sciences of Body Gunk and Sticky Green Stuff!

Dear reader,

What's your favourite bit of your body? I bet you've got one (perhaps two, if you're greedy) — or at least a bit you dislike less than the other bits. Is it your toes? Your hair? Your elbows? Go on, have a look now. A good look now — unless you're on reading this on a bus or train or something. Some people might not appreciate it...

Personally, I've got a favourite mole.

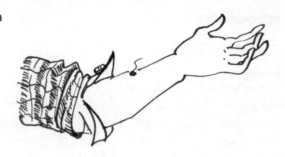

Isn't it gorgeous?

Anyway, where were we? Oh yes... whatever your favourite bit is, it's wonderful, isn't it? Think of all the useful things it does for you. You might think my mole is totally useless, but look again – it decorates my arm perfectly! And just think of all the beautiful bits of body you can't see, hidden on the insides of you...

WHAT SHALL I HAVE FOR BREAKFAST?

Lovely grey squidgy bits that think.

GLUNK
SLOOSH
GLUG

Beautiful strange multi-coloured bits that make odd noises.

6

Did you know?

The word 'snot' has been around in English for at least a thousand years (it used to be 'gesnot'!), and is also used to mean the same thing in Denmark and Norway – it probably came from the Vikings...

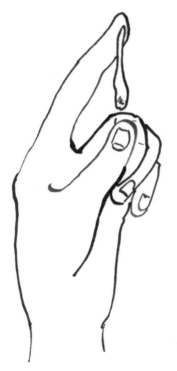

And, of course, wonderful green snotty bits that come out of your nose.

Mmm, nice.

Eurgh!

(No, don't eat it. You'll ruin your appetite.)

Still not convinced? Still don't think your body's lovely – not even the insides of your nostrils?

Shame.

You don't know what you're missing. You should get to know your body better... Perhaps even take it to church.

Yes, even the snot.

**Noooooooooooooooooo!
Not the snot!**

What, you don't think snot, or nose-picking, or sneezing, or nose-wiping have got anything to do with church or God or anything like that?
Or the Bible?

You're sure? Not even a little bit?
Well, I'm sorry, you'll just have to stop reading this book, then won't you?

**Fair enough – I've
just seen a nice book about
garden gnomes on the
next shelf...**

Because this book is about snot, about mucus, about bogies – about some of the interesting, green, yellow, gooey, sticky things that run around the insides of your body – and it's about why we've got snot, what we do with it and what God thinks about it. As you read this book, YOU will personally be able to join in and benefit from the research and work of the University of Snot in this fascinating area of human (and bogey) life! We will be asking the **Five Crucial Questions** of Advanced Snotology:

 Number 1: **Who made snot?** and Number 1-and-a-half: **Was it God?**

 Number 2: **If God made snot, why did he do it?**

 Number 3: **What is it for?**

 Number 4: **What might looking at snot tell us about other things God made?**

And   **Number 5:** **Is it time for tea yet and are we having bubble and squeak?** (OK, I won't be asking that question in this book.)

Right then. Give your nose a good blow, unwrap the tissue and have a look at it for while (lovely!), throw it away somewhere safe

and turn over the page...

Snotty Etiquette

Don't pick your nose (well, not too much)! It's not really such a great idea, because it means you might poke bits of grot and dirt further into your nose, instead of keeping them out – or worse still, you might damage the inside of your nose. If you really must pick your nose, make sure you've got clean fingers and not very long nails, and don't flick it at people! (It's not polite – and they might do it back to you!)

Do blow your nose (but not too hard)! Did you know that there's a right and a wrong way to blow your nose when you've got a cold? If you hold the handkerchief too tight around your nose and blow really hard, you won't get rid of the mucky, germ-ridden snot from your nose – instead, you might blow it into other parts of the body like the ears, where it'll lurk and do nasty things.

The trick is to hold the hankie closer to one nostril than to the other, blow (but not too hard!), and then switch over, so you empty both nostrils of all that grotty snot...

Part 1

From the Files of the
University of Snot:
A Very Important,
Highly Scientiffik
Investimagation
into

The Origins of Snot

Breathing Experiment Number One:
Things To Do With A Mouth

 Step One Find a window, one you can see out of without craning your neck.

 Step Two Stand very close to it.

 Step Three Go on, you can stand a bit closer than that... (But not too close, or you'll bash your nose, and we need it for the next experiment!)

 Step Four Open your mouth wide, as wide as you possibly can...

 Step Five Breathe in...

 Step Six ...and breathe out slowly, blowing onto the glass of the window (you can make an 'ahhh!' noise if you like, but you don't have to unless you want to).

RESULTS If it's a hot day, you might find that nothing much happens. But if it's a cold day, or a wet day, you'll see a little misty, warm, wet cloud appear on the glass there in front of you, made up of tiny drops of moisture and warm air from right inside you. And, because it's come right out of your insides, this mist is alive! Did you know that both inside and around us are zillions of tiny little living things?

You're like a giant, walking city for all kinds of germs and bacteria to make their home in. And all of them, like you, are part of the strange, fantastic world that God has made!

Breathing Experiment Number Two:
Things To Do With A Nose

 Step One — Breathe in, using only your nose this time.

 Step Two — Keep your mouth closed!

PROPERTY OF UNIVERSITY OF SNOT

 Step Three — Breathe out, still using only your nose.

Step Four — Repeat Steps 1 to 3 a few times. Listen carefully to the noises you make

WARNING! DO NOT ATTEMPT THIS EXPERIMENT IF YOU HAVE A COMPLETELY BLOCKED NOSE! YOU WILL NOT BE ABLE TO COMPLETE STEP THREE AND WILL CONK OUT IN A DEAD FAINT, WHICH IS NOT RECOMMENDED BY THE UNIVERSITY OF SNOT!
FURTHERMORE, DO NOT INTERRUPT ANYONE PERFORMING THIS EXPERIMENT! DO NOT PUT PEGS ON THEIR NOSE OR CORKS UP THEIR NOSTRILS! THIS IS A VERY SERIOUS SCIENTIFIC MATTER...

 You might have heard just a really quiet little whisper or a great loud sniff. If you've got a cold, you might have made a really odd noise: a great raging, rattling gurgle of snottiness – weeeeshorrrrrrgluglugluglugsniff!
All that noise is snot squelching about.

Try it again – actually, no, perhaps it's better if you don't. You probably ought to blow your nose first – we don't want to get snot everywhere.

Further Research: Where Did All That Breath Come From?

Snot may be gunky, but it's not just in your body to look pretty or block up your nose when you have a cold. As part of your carefully designed body, it does all kinds of useful things which help you breathe – and this is a hugely important thing for bodies to be doing!

Why is snot green and sticky?

Snot doesn't start out green – it's meant to be clear and runny, but as it does it's job of picking up germs and dust and muck in the nose and keeping them away from the rest of the body, it gets dirty. And as it gets dirty, it goes green!

That's why, when you've got a cold, it's even more green – the more green it is, the more germs and dirt in it!

So where did all this breath come from?

The Bible tells us how humans first started living and breathing. In the first story in the Bible it says that God made the first man and woman: he made the man out of a handful of soil and, later, he made the woman out of the man's rib (it may sound odd, but God can do amazing things). Then, he BREATHED into the people, and they came to life and started to breathe, too.

Breathing Experiment Number Three:
Things To Do With Some Mud

 Step One Get hold of some soil (don't bring it inside, you'll make a mess).

 Step Two Make it into the shape of your favourite creature (personally, I'm quite fond of earwigs).

 Step Three Breathe on it.

 RESULTS If you followed the experiment above accurately you will have the amazing result of... Nothing happening at all. Sorry!

We're not God, and our breath doesn't give life, although it does have things living in it.

Can you imagine what God's breath might be like, if you could see or feel it? Think of all the ways you could describe your own breath, but a thousand times better – quiet, gentle whispers; noisy, explosive snorts!

15

Hang on a minute! I'm a pretty nasty person (and my snot's not very nice to look at, either)! Why would God make me?

Sorry, I don't know the answer to that one...

Well, you're a pretty rubbish author then, aren't you?

Hang on! I hadn't finished! I was going to say that I don't know the answer to that (because it's such an enoooormous question it needs God to answer it properly), but we *do* have some clues...

Clue Number One:
God says the things he makes are good.

When God made the world, every time he finished something, he looked at it and thought:

THIS IS GOOD!

In fact, after he made men and women, he said:

THIS IS VERY GOOD!

So if God was pleased with what he had made, and said how good it was, that includes us. You can't argue with God (well, you can try, but you won't win). God didn't make us to be horrible – he made us (all of us, even the snotty bits of us) to be:

VERY GOOD!

see page 36 for more about this

Clue Number Two:
God makes things really well, and enjoys doing it.

What special skills have you got? Can you touch your nose with your tongue? I can (just!) but it makes it very hard to write. Can you play football, draw, climb things, make things or mend things? Sometimes it's just great to do the things you're really good at, and enjoy doing then as well as you can. The Bible often mentions how skilful and careful God was when he made his world, and everything in it. He obviously enjoyed it! It also talks about how God puts together babies when they're inside their mum... it talks about how carefully and how wonderfully he does it!

It's great to think of how much care and enjoyment God took to make both you and me, and everything inside us (even the snot!).

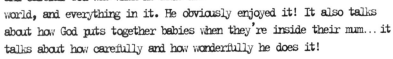

Clue Number Three:
God made us to praise him!

What God did in making you and me (and all the other things he made too) was incredibly special and tricky to do.

So special that just the fact that we exist, that every one of us is full of carefully made bits going slosh, gurgle and snort at all the right times, shows that he is an amazing God. We can look at each other and see how amazing God is!

What a particularly well-made pair of elbows!

It's like everything God has made shouts praise to him and tells the world how great he is, just by being there.

So there's something to think about, the next time you find yourself looking at a hankie full of snot.

18

Part 2

JOURNEY
TO THE
CENTRE
OF THE
NOSE!

Exploring The Nose

If you want to talk about snot in detail, you have to be ready, of course, to talk about the places where snot spends most of its time hanging out – like nostrils, sinuses and nasal passages. So let's take a look around!

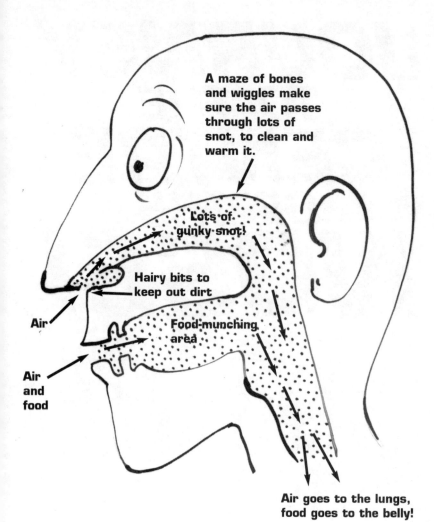

A maze of bones and wiggles make sure the air passes through lots of snot, to clean and warm it.

Lots of gunky snot!

Hairy bits to keep out dirt

Air

Food-munching area

Air and food

Air goes to the lungs, food goes to the belly!

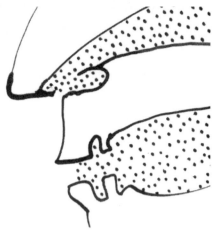

Noses are for making sure that air gets into the body and goes down into the lungs. These take important things out of the air (like oxygen), and pass them around to the rest of the body, to keep the body going.

One important thing noses do is *clean* the air that goes into the body. The other thing they do is make sure that that air is *warm* and *wet*. Snot plays an essential part in doing both those things. As we continue our journey into the nose, we'll learn more about *how* it does that...

Things To Look Out For Inside The Nose:
Good Snot And Bad Snot

When we say

snot!

we could actually mean one of two things...

1 There's one kind of snot that's always around, in your nose and other parts of your body. If I felt like showing off, I could call this kind of snot

mucus

which is what doctors and scientists call it. This kind of snot does a lot of important things.

2 When we get ill, sometimes the nose doesn't work exactly right, and the body can make too much mucus or snot, which runs out of the nose and gets in the way. This snot can have nasty gunk in it, which the body needs to get rid of as quickly as possible. If I were showing off (which of course I would never do) I could call this kind of snot

purulent nasal discharge

which is basically a more complicated way of saying 'nasty snot you get when you have a cold'.

So, snot is usually a good thing, but sometimes it gets in the way and doesn't do what it should...

Fig 1 *Good snot*   Fig 2 *Bad snot*

Did you know?

Snot doesn't just stick germs in the nose where they can't get further into the body – it's also slightly antiseptic, which means it fights and kills germs itself!

zzzzzaaaaap!

23

Exploring In More Detail –
One Way Of Explaining What Snot Does

You could think of the body as a walled town. Everybody inside
the city is safe behind their strong walls. But there are gates in
the walls, where the things the city needs to keep it going are
brought in.

Gatehouses are built with narrow passages so that people wanting
to get into the city can't just stroll right in. They need to be
carefully checked out first. The nose is like one of these gateways
for the body. The gateway needs protecting by soldiers, just as
the nose needs protecting by snot.

The soldiers stop anybody getting inside the city who is going to cause harm to the people inside. They might stop anybody who is going to cause trouble. Snot blocks rubbish from getting into our bodies.

Air sucked into the nose travels through the hairy bits at the front of the nose, and then through tight, curved passages made out of bone. It has to get past lots of snot, which lines the sides of these passages. The hairs stop big lumps getting in. The squidgy snot filters out any smaller bits of rubbish. It holds some germs or pieces of dirt there and sticks them fast, so they can't get further in.

So the snot in your nose keeps the body safe from infection and disease.

When it all goes horribly wrong!

If the body does get ill, it's as if robbers or bandits got into the city. The nose's checking and inspection system can't always keep out every germ or piece of dust and grit (and the nose isn't the only way into the body, just like a gatehouse isn't the only way into a city!).

If that happens, the king of the city (like the brain) might panic and send too many soldiers to the gateway. The soldiers would actually get in the way, and not be very helpful. In fact, they might just hang about the entrance, make a nuisance of themselves, and stop anybody getting in at all.

This is a bit like what happens when the body gets a cold – the body makes too much snot, which makes a mess and gets in the way, gunking-up the system.

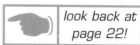

look back at page 22!

Exploring In More Detail (2) – Another Way Of Explaining What Snot Does

Snot does two things! It not only keeps nasty stuff out of the body, but it also helps keep what's in the body warm and wet. You could think of it like oil on a bicycle chain...

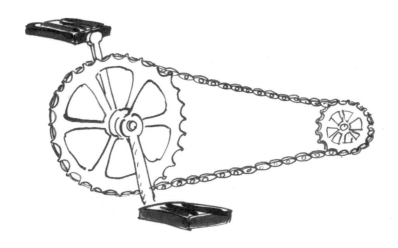

The bike has moving parts, which constantly rub against each other. If they're not kept oily, the oil dries up, and rain and air make the metals parts rusty. A rusty chain won't work properly: it won't bend as the pedals push it round and round, and it won't move smoothly over the cogs of the bike. Eventually, if it's never oiled, it'll break under the strain.

This is like how snot works in the body. From the nose, right down into the rest of the body, there are lots of tubes which pass around the food and air which the body needs to keep going. The inside of these tubes has a covering layer of snot (or 'mucus'), which protects the surface of the tube and stops it drying out – it needs to be wet and squidgy to work properly, like a bike chain needs to be oily...

The snotty lining of these tubes also keeps them snug and warm, which is helpful to the inside of the body – it doesn't like the cold!

So snot does so much more than just clog up the nose when you get a cold! Perhaps you'd better treat it with more respect, the next time you meet some...

Pleased to meet you! I'm a very important part of your body! What do you do?

Did you know?

The hairs in your nose don't just stop germs and lumps of dirt getting in, they also move the snot (mucus) along, up your nose and down into the rest of your body. Much more mucus is swallowed down inside your body than ever comes out of your nose. The reason the hairs need to move the snot around is to keep it fresh and wet and squidgy, and stop it getting hard and clogging up the glands which make more snot! This keeps your nose clean.

Believe it or not, it's actually one of the cleanest places in the body. The mouth is one of the dirtiest parts of the body
– it's full of germs and less clean than wee!

Diving Deeper: But What's The Point?

> *All this stuff bubbling and gunking and gurgling away inside me might be very impressive (and green!), but what's it got to do with God?*

Actually, what your snot does inside your body has quite a lot to do with God. That's because, when God made the world and breathed life into it and said,

THIS IS GOOD!

He didn't stop there. As we look at the bodies he made for us, we can see that they are still full of little things that show him at work:

 He gives us air to breathe into our bodies, which keeps us going.

 He made cleverly designed bodies that can fight off germs (with snot!).

And he keeps looking after those bodies today!

Just imagine...

 If you didn't have skin to stop your insides falling out!

> **Hang on, I think my intestines fell out again...**

 If you didn't have toes on the end of your feet to wiggle!

 If you didn't have elbows to do chicken impressions with!

Every bit of our body that does something useful reminds us that God cares for us, and that he hasn't stopped caring about us – he gives us what we need to live, and bodies that can protect and look after themselves!

> **See, I'm not just useful, I'm a reminder that God cares for you!**

Part 3
More Big Truths
About Snot
And *Why*
It Is How It Is

(and what God's doing about it)

Here at the University of Snot, we find it very hard to throw things away! You never know what might come in handy – only the other day we were able to patch up the University hot air balloon with some spare items from our very large collection of antique handkerchiefs!

More importantly, we keep lots of books – lists of experiments we've done, and maps of all the interesting places we've been, where we've met people and looked up their nostrils. We've kept all kinds of stories and records from the past that tell us what people knew and thought about snot! All this is important because we can use it to help us when we get stuck with difficult questions or problems.

*If God made snot to be good,
how come it's sometimes horrible,
nasty and full of disease?*

Join me on an investigation into this knotty, snotty problem, as we look through some useful books and stories, going right back to the beginning of time...

> *Why do I get a cold,*
> *and how can I get rid of it?*

No one knows *exactly* how people get runny noses, sore throats and colds. We know that germs and viruses do it, but there are so many different kinds, which all do different things!

Because there are so many germs, there's no medicine to prevent us catching it. Most colds don't last much longer than four or five days, and your body will eventually get rid of the cold itself. The best thing is to eat well (particularly things with Vitamin C in, like oranges) and to drink lots of water – because your body is using up more water than usual, making all that snot!

How it all began (again)...

In the beginning, God made all the world and everything in it. He made the heavens, the earth, the night, the day, the sky, the oceans, the land, the trees, the plants, the flowers, the sun, the moon, the stars, the fish, the birds, and all the different kind of animals – and last of all, he made people like you and me.

And their snot!

You're learning!

Anyway, where was I? Oh yes. God made everything in the world (including snot!) and it was very, very good indeed. Everything worshipped and praised him.

The sun shone, the wind blew, the fish swam, and people met with God and worshipped him. Everything was how God meant it to be, as good as it could possibly be. The things he meant to be beautiful were as beautiful as they could be, the things he meant to be useful were as useful as they could be, the things he meant to be neat and tidy were neat and tidy, and the things he meant to be messy were messy.

Even the snot was good snot, and never ever misbehaved.

But, unfortunately,
things didn't stay like that...

What Went Wrong?

In the Bible, you'll find the story of how the first man and the first woman disobeyed God by stealing and lying...

and fighting amongst themselves. Because of this, God made it so that they could no longer meet with him in the same way that they had before. People were separated from God... and nothing was ever quite so good again.

Because people no longer obeyed God, they no longer worshipped him properly – and they were no longer as good as they could possibly be. People's bodies no longer worked as well as they had before, when people obeyed God and knew him properly. People's bodies broke down, and they became ill and suffered – eventually, they died...

Like all the other bits of the body, snot no longer did exactly the job it should do. It didn't perfectly protect the rest of the body from dryness or hotness or coldness. It couldn't perfectly keep out the illness and diseases that humans started to get. Now and again people's snot itself got diseased

and caused more sickness.

see page 22–26, where we talked about the horrible stuff that snot can do when it's not working properly

What could be done? Hardly anything was working as it should! It would take a plan of genius to rescue the world from the way it was – a plan so huuuuge it would need to be a **Very Good Plan Indeed** – or perhaps a **Very God Plan Indeed**...

A Plan Is Hatched!

What happened once God's world stopped working the way he'd meant it to? It's a long story, which would take up a lot of books – more books, even, than are in the 'Why is snot green?' section of the University of Snot library...

A LONG HISTORY OF THINGS THAT ARE NOT QUITE RIGHT

NICE IDEAS THAT DIDN'T QUITE WORK

SNOT THE WAY IT SHOULD'VE BEEN
IF EVERYTHING HAD WORKED OUT ALLRIGHT

WHY CAN'T PEOPLE JUST BE NICE

People continued to disobey God and fight and lie and be cruel to each other and to the things around them. They couldn't get back to the way things had been before, when they lived with and worshipped God.

But God didn't stop loving them, and he kept showing them what he was like so that people could follow him, and try to do what he wanted. Because God had a plan...

God's Huuuuge Enormormous Amazing Rescue Plan (part 1)
What needed to be done...

All the ways people were hurting needed to be healed.

People needed to be with God again and know who he was.

People needed to be shown that God loved them, and was coming to rescue them because he loved them.

God knew that people could never come back to him by themselves - so he would go to them!

God's Huuuuge Enormormous Amazing Rescue Plan (part 2)

How God would do it...

Jesus would die and come alive again, making it possible for us to live for ever, even after our bodies have packed up!

God would make it so that people would become the perfect people (with perfect snot!) he had always wanted!

God would become a human, so he could meet with humans, face-to-face, and live with messy, snotty people like you and me, so they could learn from him how to be like he wanted them to be.

And that's what happened. God was born and was a human being,
as well as being God – Jesus.

Luke 2:1-7

Luke 9:10-17

Mark 10:13-16

John 9:1-12

Mark 7:31-37

Matthew 26:26-29

John 19:17-18

Matthew 28:8-10

43

A Quick Quiz for the Compulsively Questioning:

What Did Jesus Do?

1 How messy was Jesus?

a) Always tidy and neat! □

b) As messy as he needed to be! □

c) A total rebel – he wouldn't let anyone tell him to tidy up – *ever!* □

2 Which of these 'job descriptions' does Jesus have in the Bible?

a) teacher □
b) footballer □
c) lawyer □
d) shepherd □
e) fisherman □
f) dustman □
g) doctor □

3 How cheerful was Jesus?

a) Not at all – everything he said was
   terribly important and serious. ☐

b) He wouldn't have been serious when
   he didn't need to be – everybody has
   a laugh and a joke sometimes! ☐

c) Hysterical! He'd always be telling jokes and
   playing practical jokes on the disciples! ☐

Hold this up to a mirror to find out the answers...

1 Answer b)

see p48 for some
messy healings Jesus did!

2 Answers a), d) and g)

3 Answer b) – When Jesus talked about
God, it certainly wasn't boring! He'd often
explain what God is like with stories or jokes!
But he wasn't always joking – he knew
some things can't be joked about, and some
people need the kind of friend who isn't
always laughing...

Did Jesus have snot?

Why wouldn't he? We definitely know he had spit
(it's in the Bible!) — and snot and spit go together!
Christians don't believe that Jesus was an alien, or
a robot. He was real, and had a body like you
and me.

Jesus shows us what God wants us to be like — as
his amazing creation, but how it was always meant
to be!

Did you know?

Very early on in the story of the church, not long
after Jesus lived and died, some people went round
trying to say that Jesus was so different from
humans that he never went to the toilet! The people
who led the church were very careful to say that
that wasn't right!

Part 4

BOUNCING BACKWARDS AND FORWARDS IN TIME

To Infinity and Beyond!

God's plan doesn't stop!
God's amazing plan is still working! He wants to mend and heal the whole world – that's 2,000 years of amazing world-changing-ness since Jesus was born, and he hasn't even finished yet!

So to take a good look at it in action, and what it means for every bit of us, (including the stuff up our nostrils!) we need to travel in time...

Time: About 2,000 years ago (more or less)
Place: Jerusalem
Conditions: Muddy!

In the middle of the city of Jerusalem, there was a beggar. He lived with his mum and dad, but could not work because he had been blind since he was born. One day, he was at his usual spot by the roadside (a bit mucky and muddy, but the best he could do) when Jesus walked by.

48

Jesus' disciples didn't like the look of the grotty, horrible beggar.

Mucky from the dust of the road, unhappy, nobody to wipe his nose for him – surely to be like that God must be punishing him! Perhaps it was his parents' fault! The disciples said:

> *Why was this man born blind? Was it because he or his parents did things wrong?*

Jesus came over and sat by the beggar (who was getting a bit nervous by now). Jesus replied,

> *No, it wasn't! But because of his blindness, you will see God work a miracle for him.*

Then Jesus said:

> *While I am in the world, I am the light for the world.*

And he bent down, spat onto the earth and mixed his spit up with the earth to make *mud*, mixing it together with his hands. He took the mud and put it all over the man's eyes!

Jesus told the beggar (whose day *really* wasn't going as planned by now) to go and wash himself in a pool that was nearby. He did.

When he got back, he could see! But Jesus had gone, walking on down the road...

Keeping track of God's Plan 1
Jesus shows us that we have a God who isn't afraid of the messy mucky bits of life – he knows us inside and out (after all, he even made our snot!).

The man's eyes were healed by Jesus!

Research this in the Bible: look at John 9:1–12.

Make your own fake snot!

Ingredients
500 ml of water
3 heaped teaspoons of cornflour
1 160 ml sachet of instant un-flavoured readymade jelly flan filling
Food colouring (see suggestions below)

Wear old clothes!

Use an old saucepan (definitely not your mum's best one)!

Not toxic! (But horrible to eat!)

Get an adult to help!

How to make the snot

1 Put the saucepan on the stove and pour in the water. Slowly add the cornflour, stirring all the time to make sure it is mixed together properly.

2 Heat the mixture on a medium setting. Keep stirring regularly to stop it from becoming lumpy. Heat it for about 5–10 minutes – don't let the mixture bubble or boil. Stir it and turn the heat down if it begins to do so at any point.

3 When the mixture has become thick and looks a little clearer, remove it from the heat. Add the contents of the flan filling sachet, stirring all the time. Keep stirring the mixture for a while, to make sure the flan filling is properly mixed in.

4 Stir in some food colouring, if you want to (see below). Pour the mixture into an old jam jar or durable plastic container, and leave it to cool for at least an hour. After the snot has cooled, you can keep it for about three days, if you keep the container sealed.

5 Find some things to do with your sticky, messy fake snot – as long as you've got somewhere safe where you can make a mess with it! (Or you could just leave it in your jam jar and admire it in all its beauty!)

Colouring suggestions
Experiment with using different food colourings – either yellow or green – to get different kinds of snotty colours. A very small amount of turmeric spice can also make a good yellowy colour or change a dark green to a convincing icky, sickly green! You could also just leave the mixture as it is, without colouring, like snot is before it picks up any germs...

boing!

Time: A few years ago
Place: Not very far away from here
Conditions: Spotlessly clean (because it's a hospital!)

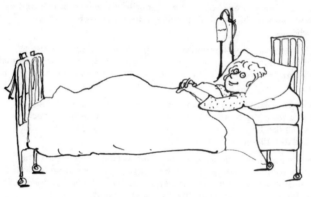

Beth was six years old. She had been ill for quite a while, and had been in hospital for ages. She had a rare illness that affected her heart and made it difficult for her to run around or do most of the things she wanted to do. Sometimes it made her very faint indeed. The doctors who tried to help her didn't know what to do. They'd tried lots of different medicines, but nothing seemed to work.

The doctors and nurses didn't stop trying to fix Beth's heart, even though it seemed difficult. But sometimes it seemed that Beth might not live very long, or be able to do very much at all when she grew up.

Beth's mum was often with her at the hospital, and because she believed in Jesus, she would pray and talk to him about Beth. She would ask God to protect Beth and look after her. But Beth's mum and Beth's friends still worried about Beth. They didn't know what God wanted to do.

One day, Beth's mum was praying, telling God how scared she was for Beth. As she prayed, she thought she heard God say:

Trust me, I know what's right. Trust me with Beth.

Although she was scared, Beth's mum told God she would trust him, whatever happened. From then on, although Beth was still ill, her mum didn't worry.

Gradually, Beth got better, although she had to go to hospital a lot. The doctors were still trying their hardest to make Beth better, but didn't know if she would be able to run about, or play with her friends too much – they were worried that she might have to spend a lot of time in bed or sitting down. Each time she came into the hospital, they would run special tests on her and look at her heart to see how it was.

Beth is much older now – the last time she went to hospital for a check-up on her heart was a long time ago. The doctors told her that her heart was completely healthy!

Why won't God make me better and make my cold go away NOW?

God *is* healing you – it will take a little while!

Your body, with its snot and all the other bits and things inside of you was designed to fight germs. And that is what it is doing – healing you! And God made it to be that way – you just have to be patient.

We know that God does sometimes make 'miraculous' healings happen – but there's always a reason for it. Perhaps the person who needs healing has been suffering for a long time, or God wants to make a big point, which the illness or the problem the person has is just part of...

see page 55 for
more messy healing!

Keeping track of God's Plan 2
God's love for us keeps on going, all the time protecting us from diseases and illness – sometimes its very obvious, but sometimes it's quite amazing stuff that nobody expects!

boing!

Time: About 2,000 years ago (more or less)
Place: Somewhere in ancient Israel
Conditions: Crowded!

Jesus was travelling about with his disciples again. Crowds came from all around to see him, because they had heard about him and came to hear him speak about God, or see him heal people.

Can you see what's going on?

Move your head!

Some people who lived nearby heard that Jesus was coming, and brought out to him a friend of theirs who was deaf and could not speak. They knew he needed healing, and begged Jesus:

Please, put your hand on him!

Jesus took the man who could not speak or hear, and they went somewhere away from the crowd. Jesus put his fingers in the man's ears, then he spat and touched the man's tongue. He looked up to heaven, and said to the man,

Open up!

Immediately, the man could hear, and could talk – his friends could understand him easily!

Research this in the Bible: look at Mark 7:31-37

Did you know?

Most people's bodies make about 250 ml of snot a day! That's about 7 litres (or three and a half coke bottles) every month!

Bodies make even more spit than that – about a litre (half a coke bottle) every day!

boing!

Time: Not very long ago
Place: Still not very far away (by the roadside)
Conditions: Bumpy!

Rob sat by the side of the road, feeling scared and confused. His bike was lying on its side in the road, and people were running out of their houses to see what had happened. He'd been cycling downhill as fast as he could, on his way to meet a friend. Suddenly there was a lot of blood everywhere (mainly on him!) and his mouth hurt a lot. What had happened?

Rob's feet had missed the pedals for a second as he cycled. The bike had skidded, and he'd suddenly fallen forward very hard. As he'd fallen, he'd bitten through his lip – so hard that he'd broken some of his front teeth (so it's not surprising it hurt!).

He didn't stay sitting on the side of the road for long, though. Someone called for an ambulance, and he was soon being taken off to hospital. At the hospital, the doctors and nurses gave Rob an injection to keep his mouth numb and make it hurt less. They cleaned out the cut and got rid of little bits of tooth that were in it. They made sure they did a really good job!

Then they stitched up Rob's lip. By that time, it was starting to swell, because it was bruised and hurting. The next morning, when he woke up, it was huuuge! For the next few days, Rob had difficulty talking to anyone – and at meals, he had to drink soup through a straw! But by the end of the week, the swelling had gone down enough for him to go to the dentist and have his teeth repaired.

Keeping Track of God's Plan 4

God's plan to heal the world isn't just about God taking over and making things right without people being involved. It wouldn't be a very good plan if it was like that. He wants us to take part, too! Just like doctors and nurses help people get better, he wants us to care for people and look after them...

I needed so many people to help me when I fell off my bike – and it wasn't a really nasty accident, like if I'd broken my arm, or anything! I'm so glad that there are people in God's world who want to help people to be healed!

But at the time, he just said,

Thag you berry buch!

The University of Snot: All you Really Need To Know

If you've enjoyed reading this book, you might like to go on and study at the University of Snot – but most of you are probably too young to do that now. So, especially for you, the reader, I personally present you with 'The Essential Principles Of Advanced Snotology' for you to remember and keep, summarising the key things you need to know about snot. You never know when they might come in handy!

But watch out! As a qualified Advanced Snotologist, you might find you keep looking at the things God has made and asking questions about them and what they say about God – you never know where it might lead!

Did you know?

The ancient Egyptians had their own hieroglyphic symbol for colds and sniffles – it looked a bit like a nose...

Five Fantastic Things You Really Ought To Know About Snot:

1 It's not really gross or disgusting at all! It's part of your body, so don't be rude to it.

2 It's made by your body to do useful jobs:
Keeping your nose and body clean and free from dirt, germs and bacteria.
Keeping the rest of your body working smoothly and gloopily (because gloopy and sticky is good for bodies).

3 Even when you get a cold, your body is working to get better.

4 Snot is just one of a *huuuuuuuge* number of different thingies and groups of thingies that work to protect your body and make the things it does good things.

5 It's made by God and so are you!

Five Fantastic Things About God, The Maker Of Snot:

1 He loves *every bit* of us, even the messy bits – that's why he
made us with bodies that look after themselves.

2 He knows us better than we know ourselves (even the messy
bits!).

3 He is not scared of the gloopy, messy things we might think are
gross or disgusting (like snot!). He isn't afraid to get involved
in the messy stuff to make his amazing plans work out.

4 Jesus is God come to meet us – he doesn't run away from us,
shouting, "URRRRRGH! GET IT AWAY FROM ME!" He comes to
us (messy bits and all), and helps us understand him.

5 Bodies might not work properly all the time, but God wants to
heal us – inside and out – and he's working all the time to
do that.

_____

has studied for a Qualification In Green Sticky Stuff

at the

University of Snot!

They are allowed to call themselves an Advanced

Snotologist, for they have learnt many important things

about bogeys and mucus, and why they are an important

part of the world God has made!

Signed:

Professor Abednego Smott

This book is dedicated to Jackie, with love and appreciation,
in the hope that it may give some insight into the strange ideas
that crawl out of my head now and again.

Enormous green stringy thanks to everybody who's helped me
with ideas and writing and thinking and deadline-chasing, notably
Amy (whose fault it was), Carsten (with the snotty attitude),
John (for hard, crunchy facts) and Lizzie (ta!). Numerous other
larger-than-life heroes and heroines should feature in the halls of
fame of the University of Snot – you're all great (and probably
mad)!

Essential thanks to Anne and all of the SU Children's Team for
their nurture, faith and hard work, without which this book
would not exist. The same goes for my family, without the same
from whom I would not exist.